PIPER MORGAN
IN CHARGE!

DON'T MISS PIPER'S OTHER ADVENTURES!

Piper Morgan Joins the Circus

COMING SOON:

Piper Morgan to the Rescue

Piper Morgan Makes a Splash!

ALSO BY STEPHANIE FARIS:

30 Days of No Gossip

25 Roses

PIPER MORGAN

IN CHARGE!

BY STEPHANIE FARIS
ILLUSTRATED BY LUCY FLEMING

♡

ALADDIN
New York   London   Toronto   Sydney   New Delhi

ALADDIN
An imprint of Simon & Schuster Children's Publishing Division
1230 Avenue of the Americas, New York, New York 10020
First Aladdin hardcover edition August 2016
Text copyright © 2016 by Stephanie Faris
Illustrations copyright © 2016 by Lucy Fleming
Also available in an Aladdin paperback edition.
All rights reserved, including the right of reproduction in whole or in part in any form.
ALADDIN is a trademark of Simon & Schuster, Inc., and related logo is a registered trademark of Simon & Schuster, Inc.
For information about special discounts for bulk purchases, please contact Simon & Schuster Special Sales at 1-866-506-1949 or business@simonandschuster.com.
The Simon & Schuster Speakers Bureau can bring authors to your live event. For more information or to book an event contact the Simon & Schuster Speakers Bureau at 1-866-248-3049 or visit our website at www.simonspeakers.com.
Book designed by Laura Lyn DiSiena
The text of this book was set New Baskerville.
Manufactured in the United States of America 0716 FFG
2 4 6 8 10 9 7 5 3 1
Library of Congress Control Number 2016932238
ISBN 978-1-4814-5712-5 (hc)
ISBN 978-1-4814-5711-8 (pbk)
ISBN 978-1-4814-5713-2 (eBook)

For Hollis, the inspiration for every young character I write

CHAPTER
★ 1 ★

I usually love the first day of school.

Only it was March instead of September. And I was going to a new school, not my old one.

And my mom would be working there.

We were staying with my nanna because my mom got a new job. Just a few weeks ago she was working in the circus, where there were elephants and clowns and lots of fun things.

But then Mom got this new job where she'd be working in the principal's office, helping out with a big project they were doing, and other office-y things. It did not sound as fun as seeing Ella the Elephant every day. And I don't think there will be clowns in the principal's office, but Nanna said I could be wrong about that.

"Piper! Breakfast!" Mom yelled.

I grabbed my new, pink sparkly backpack and bounced my way to the kitchen. I bounce when I'm excited about something, and I'm super-duper excited about Nanna's breakfast. She makes pancakes with bananas baked right into them. Plus, she has hot syrup.

"Don't you just look all bright and shiny, Piper." Nanna smiles.

If Nanna thought my smiling face was

bright and shiny, wait until she saw my backpack. I grinned. That was the shiniest part of my whole outfit—and my favorite. I saw the pancakes and squeezed into my chair, backpack and all.

"No backpacks at the table," my mom said from behind me. "Pancakes. Yummy. We can't eat like this every morning, though."

I put my backpack on the floor next to me. But I made sure my foot touched it. That way I'd know if Oreo tried to take it. Oreo is Nanna's puppy. He's named Oreo because he's black and white, like Oreo cookies.

"Mom," I said, after swallowing my first big bite of pancakes. "Can I ride the school bus?"

"No, Piper," Mom said. She gave Nanna a look. When two

grown-ups look at each other like that, it's like they're talking about you without talking.

"Your mom's driving you to school today," Nanna said as she brought over the last plateful of pancakes she'd made. "Maybe you'll be able to be your mom's helper. Won't that be fun?"

"A helper like you were in the circus," Mom explained. "You had fun doing that, right, Piper? And you might make some new friends. First you have to go to class, though."

I actually had liked it when Mom was working for the circus. Besides meeting all the animals and clowns, I was part of the Little Explorers—a bunch of the other kids whose moms and dads worked for the circus too—and even though I wasn't the greatest dancer or ringleader, I still had a lot of fun.

"I would be a good helper," I said.

Mom leaned forward to give me a quick kiss on the forehead. "You were so good with the other kids in the circus, the principal might let you help in the office when he hears about it."

That news was good enough to make me set my fork down. I bounced up and down in my chair, but just a little. Not enough to make the chair move.

"Yay!" I said. "Can I answer phones?" I could picture myself in a big chair, answering Very Important Phone Calls.

Mom and Nanna looked at each other and shared one of those *isn't she cute?* smiles. *Isn't she cute?* smiles are my favorite kinds of smiles.

"We'll see, Piper," Mom said. "Come on, let's go to your first day of school!"

Class Fact #1

The first school bus ever was a horse-drawn carriage. That means you climbed in the back of the cart and a horse pulled you all the way to school. It was called a "kid hack" because "hack" is short for "hackney carriage."

Some kid hacks had one long bench on each side, so all the kids rode to school facing the kids on the other bench. You climbed in from the back so that you wouldn't scare the horses. That meant you couldn't pet the horses either, which would have been the fun part about having a horse pull you to school.

Still, buses with engines are better. Mostly because they have air conditioners and heaters.

CHAPTER ★ 2 ★

My eyes got wide as Mom drove into the parking lot of my new school. It was humongous. My last school was just a small one. Mom said that was because this school was four billion miles from Nanna's house, and a lot of the other towns near Nanna had kids who went to this school too. I don't think it was really four billion miles. That would take at least an hour to drive. We only drove for exactly forty-two minutes.

"Even though it looks big, Piper, don't be nervous," Mom said, squeezing my hand. "I think you are going to like it here."

Inside, the school looked even bigger. There were really high ceilings and big windows, with lots of art and cool posters everywhere.

"Come on, Piper," Mom said as I stopped to take a look at a flower picture. "We need to go to the principal's office to get you all settled."

The principal's office was a small area at the front of the school. A principal's office wasn't a good place to be unless your mom worked there. Then it was fun.

When we first walked in, I saw a girl sitting in one of the chairs. In my old school those were the trouble chairs. When you got in trouble, you had to wait there until the principal came out and got you. I only had to sit in those chairs once, and it was because Pauly Nichols was making fun of me. When I decided to tease him right back, the principal thought it was "fighting." I said I was just making things even.

This girl didn't look happy. I decided I'd be nice to her. Maybe she'd feel better if I told her a funny story.

"Wait here," Mom said, pointing to the trouble chairs.

I frowned. I didn't want to wait in the trouble chairs. People would think I was in trouble.

But then I remembered the girl. She

needed someone to make her feel better. I plopped down next to her.

"Hi," I said. "I'm Piper Morgan. I got in trouble once too."

"I'm not in trouble," she told me.

"Oh."

"He's my dad."

She was pointing to the door that had a sign on it. PRINCIPAL, the black letters on the gold sign told me.

Principal. Principals could be dads?

"I'm his helper bee," the girl boasted. "Watch."

The girl hopped up and ran over to a door that flipped away when she pushed on it. That let her go behind the desk. Only I couldn't see her anymore.

I got up and followed her.

The flippy door was easy to push open. Too easy, I guess. I flipped it and it came back to me, almost hitting me. I had to jump back.

Once I got past the door, I was behind the desk. I was back there, like someone who worked there.

"Lily, what are you doing back here?" a woman asked. I couldn't see anyone at first, but then I saw a woman with pink hair. Pink hair! I didn't even see that in the circus.

"Working," the girl who was the principal's daughter said. She must be Lily. Lily couldn't reach the counter, though, so working was just standing on her tippy-toes and stretching really far to try to reach the stapler.

"Chairs help you reach things," I told Lily. I found a roll-y chair and pulled it over. "They make you taller."

I'd learned that at my house. Sometimes when Mom was doing something, she'd pull a chair over and stand on it to get things out of high cabinets. Like cereal. Or bowls. Or the Play-Doh.

Only, I forgot one thing when I was pulling the chair over. Chairs in houses don't have wheels. Chairs in offices sometimes do. It makes them easier to roll around, but not so easy to stand on.

I started to get up on the chair, but then it got all roll-y. I fell back into the chair and squaled as I went *whoosh* all the way across the floor. It was so fun.

But then something bad happened. The chair slammed into a big cabinet of papers and files, and things went flying all over the place. The chair stopped, but it was too late. It had already made the biggest mess ever.

I heard the principal's office door open right as the pink-haired lady appeared, her eyebrows all squiggled with concern.

"She did it!" I heard Lily yell out.

Class Fact #2

Standing on a chair is a super dangerous thing to do. Even if that chair doesn't have wheels. Here's some of the bad stuff that can happen:

#1 YOU COULD FALL.

#2 YOU COULD DROP THE THING YOU HAVE IN YOUR HAND.

#3 THAT THING COULD BE A DOUGHNUT. OR CHOCOLATE MILK.

#4 YOU COULD MAKE LOTS OF NOISE AND GET IN LOTS OF TROUBLE.

#5 ACTUALLY, YOU COULD GET IN REALLY BIG TROUBLE FOR ALL OF THE ABOVE.

CHAPTER
★ 3 ★

Going to the principal's office is easy when you're already there. You don't even have to wait in a trouble chair.

After I knocked all those important papers over, my mom sat me down in the principal's office and said I couldn't move until she came back.

"No more chair shenanigans," she said. She was a lot meaner than the principal, who actually winked at me after Mom finished being mad at me.

They left me sitting in Mr. Steadman's office, alone. I couldn't leave my chair— Mom said not to—but I could lean forward really far and see what was on a principal's desk. A file folder with the words "Morgan, Piper" on it.

That was my name! Backward, but still my name.

I reached my arms out as far as I could and slid the folder across the desk. It had my name on it, so that meant I could read it, right? Plus, I hadn't left my seat so I was still following the rules. Maybe once I read the file, I could find out what we had to do to stay here a long time.

See, if Mom could keep this job forever and ever, that meant I could stay here and make friends. Not Lily, though. Lily wasn't nice.

Inside the folder was a piece of paper with stuff about me all over it. My name, my age—things like that. Nothing about my mom's job or how long we got to stay. I couldn't read much, though, because I heard voices outside the door. But I turned the page and saw a piece of paper beneath that said, "Helper bee?" in big letters, surrounded by doodles.

Helper bee! I liked that.

Smiling, I shut the folder and put it right back on the desk where I'd found it. If I was good, I could be a helper bee. And I knew exactly what that meant. I'd be a better helper bee than Lily was and I could stay in the school. If you were really good at helping out, they'd want you to keep helping.

When the door opened, Mr. Steadman came back in with a big grin on his face. I decided I liked this principal.

"Are you sure you're okay?" he asked. "We can get the school nurse."

"I'm okay," I said. I wanted to let out a great big sigh, since they'd asked me that too many times already. But the principal was being nice, so I held my sigh inside.

"We're going to put you in Miss Nutter's class," Mr. Steadman said. "You'll like her."

I wondered if Miss Nutter would be as nice as Miss Sarah was to me in the circus. Miss Sarah was a ballerina, and she helped me out a lot when I was a part of the Little Explorers. "Is Miss Nutter a ballerina?" I asked Mr. Steadman.

"Huh?" he asked. "No. I don't think so.

Why don't we go meet her and you can ask her yourself?"

"Can I really?" I asked the principal as we walked from his office to Miss Nutter's classroom. I don't think he heard me. He didn't ever answer my question.

My big smile went right off my face when I saw Miss Nutter. She seemed nice, but she was nothing like Miss Sarah. Miss Sarah was young and tall and ballerina-like. Miss Nutter was short and lots of years older than even my mom. And that was *old*.

"Well, this must be our new pupil," Miss Nutter said. I didn't know what a "pupil" was, but I didn't have time to ask. That's because Miss Nutter took my hand and rushed me into the classroom, where she made me stand in front of everyone while she introduced me.

"Everyone, this is our new pupil, Piper Morgan. Please make her feel welcome here. Piper once helped out in a circus. Isn't that fun, everyone?"

Hands immediately shot up in the air. They wanted to ask me questions! I looked at Miss Nutter, hoping she'd call on someone.

"Yes, Jeska?" Miss Nutter asked.

A girl near the front lowered her hand. "Umm, were there animals and stuff?"

"Yes," I said. "There were elephants and monkeys. They were so fun."

"Matthew?" Miss Nutter asked.

"Were the clowns scary?" the boy next to Jeska asked.

"Not at all," I said. "They were super nice."

"Katherine?" Miss Nutter asked.

"Will you sit with us at lunch?" she asked.

I smiled and nodded. I didn't need Lily to be nice to me. I had friends already.

Miss Nutter turned to me. "Piper, why don't you go sit down at the desk right there? And you will have a great desk buddy for the year."

She made me sit at my new desk, which was right at the front of the room. But that wasn't the worst part.

The worst part was that my desk buddy—the girl sitting right next to me—was Lily from the office.

Class Fact #3

In the early 1800s, not every child went to school, as it was only for very rich people. A man named Horace Mann thought *all* kids should be able to go, so he fought to make sure they could. He created the Common Schools Movement, which made sure every kid knew the three *R*s: Reading, Writing, and Arithmetic.

(Two of those words don't start with *R*. I wonder if anyone told them that.)

There are kids in the world who can't go to school and learn because they don't live near one, or have to work to help their families.

Think about that the next time you don't want to get on the bus, or when you don't feel like doing your homework!

CHAPTER ★ 4 ★

I didn't want to talk about school.
I just wanted to sit and eat my dinner. And pet Oreo.

"Piper," Mom said. "Hands above the table."

No petting dogs at the table. That was a rule here. It was Mom's rule, not Nanna's.

"Tell us about your first day of school, Piper," Nanna said. "Did you make any new friends?"

"Mm-hmm," I said. My mouth had potatoes in it so I couldn't say any words.

I got to sit with my new friends Jeska and Matthew and Katherine—who went by Katie—at lunch. They were all the best kinds of friends you could find. *Nice* friends.

Lily had sat near us too, with her friend Mouse, but they did not say anything to me.

"Piper may get to be a helper bee, but only if she behaves," Mom explained. "Helper bees do fun things, like help take papers to teachers."

"Wow," Nanna said. "That sounds like an important job."

"There's a very nice girl named Lily," Mom told Nanna. "She works in the principal's office too. They're going to work together on a special project."

My eyes got very big as I swallowed the potatoes and looked at Mom. Working together? Me and Lily? That wasn't part of the deal.

"I can't work with her," I told Mom. "She's mean."

"Piper!" Mom said.

"What did she do?" Nanna asked Mom.

"Piper got in trouble for playing with a chair," Mom answered. "Lily told on her."

"And tattling isn't nice," I said.

Mom looked at me then. "Tattling is okay if it keeps someone from getting hurt," she said. "And what you did could have gotten you hurt. Do you understand that?"

This was one of those "very special lessons," I had a feeling. I didn't have time for that.

"No trying to stand on chairs," I said. "Especially if they have roll-y things on the bottom."

"Wheels?" Nanna asked.

"Can't I just work alone?" I asked Mom. "I'll learn more that way."

Mom shook her head. "Mr. Steadman is excited about it. He says Lily knows the school and you bring new energy. You're the perfect team."

I ran my fork through my mashed potatoes over and over. I wanted to eat enough to get dessert, but my appetite wasn't there anymore.

"I know!" Nanna suddenly said. "You could take some cookies to Mr. Steadman. That would make you a good little helper bee. How about you and me make a batch for tomorrow?"

I looked up at Nanna. That was it! That would do it! I could work together with Lily and still be Mr. Steadman's favorite helper bee, even if Lily was his daughter. Especially once Mr. Steadman tasted the best chocolate chip cookies ever.

I smiled at Nanna. Nannas sure have some great ideas.

Class Fact #4

Did you know that having dinner with your family is important? It makes you smarter, happier, and healthier. Here are some fun facts about family dinners:

#1 KIDS WHO EAT WITH THEIR PARENTS A LOT ARE MORE LIKELY TO GET GOOD GRADES ON THEIR REPORT CARDS.

#2 KIDS WHO EAT WITH THEIR PARENTS GET TO TALK ABOUT HOW GREAT THEIR DAY AT SCHOOL WAS.

#3 YOU DON'T HAVE TO HAVE A FANCY DINNER TO HAVE A FAMILY DINNER. EVEN PIZZA COUNTS IF YOU EAT IT AT THE SAME TABLE AND TALK TO ONE ANOTHER WHILE YOU EAT. (BUT NOT WITH YOUR MOUTH FULL.)

#1 IF YOU WATCH TV OR PLAY GAMES WHILE YOU EAT, IT DOESN'T COUNT AS A FAMILY DINNER.

CHAPTER
★ 5 ★

The next day I went into the office with a round tub of Nanna's special chocolate chip cookies.

"It's for Mr. Steadman," I'd whispered to Miss Cindy, the pink-haired school secretary. She sat at the front desk in the office. "I want to show him I'm the best helper bee."

"All helper bees are the best, Piper," Miss Cindy said, but she smiled and took the cookies, putting them on her desk.

Mr. Steadman was busy, so Miss Cindy told me to go to class until recess. During class I sat at my desk and didn't make a peep. When it was time to line up for recess, I got in my place and didn't beg to be first. I was on my very best behavior.

That would make me the principal's favorite. Even though Miss Cindy thought principals didn't have favorites, I knew they did.

During recess I went back to the office. I hadn't heard anything about the new project Mom told me about, but maybe that would happen after school. I'll bet helper bees did lots of stuff after school, since there was not much time in the morning.

Lily was already sitting in a chair near the door. I gave her a wave, but she just kept looking at the floor. It was okay—I was too excited about my first job as a helper bee to be mad at Lily. I wore a big smile as I went up to Miss Cindy's desk.

But my smile went *poof* when I saw that her desk was missing something.

Nanna's tub of cookies was gone! "Miss Cindy!" I called out. "Have you seen my tub of cookies that I had this morning?"

Miss Cindy frowned. "I haven't seen them since you were here earlier, Piper," she said. "I thought I put them on my desk. I'll ask Mr. Steadman if he's seen them."

She went over to Mr. Steadman's office, but I had a strange feeling Lily had something to do with the missing cookies. After all, she'd gotten to the office ahead of me and was sitting in the trouble chair, quiet as a mouse, not saying a word.

"Okay, everyone, let's see what's going on," Mr. Steadman said as he came out of his office. "They have to be here some-where. Did you look in the mail slots?"

"Mail slots?" I asked. "They were in a big plastic tub."

It was pretty and light pink and had a cover. Nanna wouldn't be happy when I told her that her bowl was gone too. It was her favorite.

"Maybe someone took them out," Miss Cindy said.

"Or maybe someone ate them," I said.

I looked right at Lily then. I did it so that both Mr. Steadman and Miss Cindy could see. Mom says you should never, ever point, so I pointed with my eyes. Just like *that*.

They both looked at her. I think they got my super-secret message.

"Lily," Mr. Steadman said. "Can you come over here for a second?"

Lily hopped up all of a sudden and walked to the copy machine. She acted like she couldn't hear us, but I knew she could. She wasn't fooling me at all.

"I'm busy," Lily said. She pushed a button and the copier went *whoosh*.

"Now!" Mr. Steadman said in an *I mean business, young lady* kind of voice.

Lily walked over to us, her hands behind her back. She swayed when she walked. I think she was doing that on purpose.

"Let me see your hands," her dad said.

Lily put her hands in front of her and behind her back again. And that was when I knew she was G-U-I-L-T-Y with a capital *G*. She didn't have a cookie in her hands, but what was she hiding back there?

"Lily?" Mr. Steadman asked.

I thought of something then. What if your

dad was a principal? I don't know if I would like that. Principals were scary, even if they were smiley principals like Mr. Steadman.

"Hands," Mr. Steadman ordered.

Looking down at the ground, Lily put her hands in front of her again. Her dad leaned over and looked at them, but I was down that low already. I saw what Mr. Steadman was seeing before he saw it.

There was chocolate on her hands.

I knew it! Lily *had* eaten Nanna's cookies!

Class Fact #5

There are some easy ways to tell if someone is lying. Want to know what they are?

#1 SHE WON'T MAKE EYE CONTACT.
EVEN WHEN YOU TELL HER TO, SHE
LOOKS LIKE SHE CAN'T WAIT TO
LOOK AWAY.

#2 SHE FIDGETS.

#3 SHE DOESN'T MOVE AT ALL. SHE
JUST STANDS REALLY, REALLY STILL.
LIKE IF SHE MOVES, YOU'LL HEAR THE
LIES SWISHING AROUND IN HER BRAIN.

#1 HER VOICE GETS REALLY HIGH
PITCHED. OR LOW PITCHED.

#5 SHE HAS EVIDENCE ON HER
HANDS.

CHAPTER
★ 6 ★

Lily was in T-R-O-U-B-L-E. And because the principal was also her dad, that meant she was in trouble times two.

It also meant I was the principal's favorite helper bee. For now, anyway.

Lily and Mr. Steadman were in his office for a long, long time. That made me the only helper bee.

I knew this was my big chance. I had to show Mr. Steadman I was the best helper bee ever so that I could be a part of the team of "bees" for good. So when Miss Cindy told me to run a note to Miss Carver's class, that's exactly what I did. I *ran*.

"No running in the hall!" one of the teachers yelled as I sped past her classroom.

I probably should have stopped then. But that teacher didn't know how important this was. I had to do it the fastest ever so that I could prove I was the best. I *was* the best message-to-Miss-Carver's-class runner ever. I was there in not too many seconds.

Miss Carver's door was open so I just ran right in. I stopped my feet from running just inside the door, but my shoes were slippery, so I slid even after I'd stopped. Miss Carver held out her hands to stop me from sliding right into her.

"Well!" Miss Carver said. "That's what I'd call a delivery!"

See? Best office worker ever.

Now that I was finished, I had to go to class. Mr. Steadman said so. But I made sure Mr. Steadman would know.

"Tell Miss Cindy I'm the best helper bee ever?" I asked Miss Carver.

Her eyes were wide, but she nodded. She'd tell her. I knew she would.

Miss Nutter didn't think I was fast. She thought I was late. I explained to her that I had a very special delivery for Miss Carver's class on my way here, but she said next time I should get a late pass. "Ha!" Lily said as I sat down next to her. She actually said that. Out loud. I looked up to see if Miss Nutter had heard, but Miss Nutter was busy writing on the whiteboard.

"Give me back my bowl!" I whispered. A whisper didn't make it sound scary, though.

I knew Lily had eaten Nanna's cookies. She got in trouble for that. But she kept saying she had eaten only one and the rest had just disappeared, bowl and all. Cookies and bowls don't just disappear.

"I don't have it!" Lily snapped back. Only she didn't whisper. And Miss Nutter heard.

"Ahem," she said from the front of the class. She'd stopped writing and now was staring at us. This was when she'd write our names on the whiteboard for not being good.

"Sorry, Miss Nutter," Lily said. She smiled big too, showing lots of teeth.

Miss Nutter nodded and turned back to writing on the board.

I looked from Miss Nutter to Lily, all shocked. Lily just got away with talking in class. Nobody got away with talking in class. It must be because the principal is her dad.

Oh no. That meant that Lily could do whatever she wanted. Even hiding Nanna's bowl and not telling me where it was. I couldn't do anything about it.

Except tell the principal. The principal would see what happened and make Lily give the bowl back. I'd just have to talk to him.

Class Fact #6

Before whiteboards and fancy SMART Boards, there were these things called chalkboards. They were black and sometimes green, and you wrote on them with white chalk. They were used for hundreds of years.

You don't see chalkboards much anymore, but you can sometimes find them in toy stores. You can even buy different colors of chalk and draw pretty pictures.

CHAPTER ★ 7 ★

Mom was in the office after school.
That was good. I liked being with my mom.
But what was bad was that I couldn't find
Miss Cindy anywhere.

She wasn't at the copier.

She wasn't in Mr. Steadman's office.

She wasn't even hiding under the big table
where she sorted mail and stuff. I checked.

I needed to talk to someone about Nanna's
bowl. Only I couldn't talk to Mom, because

she'd say I shouldn't have lost Nanna's bowl and it's the most important bowl ever and didn't she tell me that Nanna's had that bowl since lots and lots of years ago?

"What's wrong, Piper?" Mom asked when she saw me.

I guess I was frowning. I turned my frown upside down and said, "Nothing," with the biggest smile ever. The kind of smile that Lily had given Miss Nutter. It had gotten Lily out of trouble, so it should keep me out of trouble too, right?

"Mr. Steadman told me what happened this morning," Mom said. She set down the stack of stuff she was holding and turned to face me. "Do you think Lily ate your cookies?"

"Yes," I said, hoping she wouldn't ask about the bowl.

Mom was quiet.

"She took my bowl, too," I added.

Wait, where had that come from? I wasn't going to say that. Now I'd blown it.

I heard the door open behind me right as Mom said, "You're saying you lost Nanna's favorite bowl? The one she said she didn't want to let you borrow because it was really important?"

"Lily stole it," I said.

"Did not!"

That was Lily, who must have been the one who had opened the office door behind me while we were talking. She was standing behind me, hands on her hips. And she was M-A-D.

"Did too!" I yelled back.

"Did not!" she yelled louder.

"Piper!" Mom said, even though Lily

was yelling too. "Lily, why don't you tell me what happened."

"She left the cookies there," Lily said. "Miss Cindy said I couldn't have one because they were for my dad. I took one."

"One?" Mom asked.

"No!" I said.

"Piper." Mom gave me one of her *I mean business* looks before turning back to Lily. "How many cookies did you eat?"

"One," Lily said. "And a bite of another one, but it wasn't a whole one."

"And then what happened?" Mom asked.

"I—I—"

Mom crossed her arms over her chest. That was the pose she used when she said things like, *I'm waiting.* That look always made me tell the truth.

"Lily?" Mom said, when Lily still didn't speak up.

Lily's bottom lip started to quiver. This was when she was going to tell the truth, I knew it. This was when she'd admit she took the cookies and everyone would get mad at her and she'd be punished, for sure.

This was when a tear rolled down Lily's cheek. Uh-oh.

"It was such a good idea," Lily said quietly. "And it wasn't fair because everyone was going to think Piper was the best helper bee, but I've been here longer. I want to be the best helper bee."

"Where did you put the cookies, Lily?" Mom asked gently.

"I didn't steal them," Lily said. "I hid them in one of the classrooms."

"It sounds like you two have a problem

to solve," Mom said. "It's a shame, too, because Mr. Steadman has a fun new project for you. But until you get Nanna's bowl, you can't do it."

I gave Lily a mean look. Great. Now we had to get the bowl before we could actually start the project!

"Why don't you two go get Nanna's cookie bowl?" Mom asked. "If you work together *without fighting*, I'll talk to Mr. Steadman about letting you still be helper bees. But you have to work together."

I wanted to help Mr. Steadman. I wanted everyone to see that I could do big-girl projects without messing them up. I wanted Mr. Steadman to see I was the best helper bee ever.

Maybe I still could. I just had to play nice with Lily first.

Class Fact #7

People think of the principal as the person who punishes you when you're in trouble. But the principal is super important.

Did you know that the principal is the boss of all the teachers?

Did you know that the principal can make rules that everyone has to follow?

Did you know that if you have something you need to talk about, you can go to the principal's office and he or she will help you?

That makes the principal pretty great.

CHAPTER ★ 8 ★

"I don't remember!"

I sighed. Once we'd left the office, Lily started playing a new game. It was called, "I don't remember where I put the bowl."

Only, I knew she had to remember. It had been only a few hours since she had put it in the mystery classroom. It was silly to look for the bowl when Lily knew where it was.

We looked in Miss Nutter's classroom.

We looked in Miss Carver's classroom.

We looked in all the other classrooms too.

We were trying to get into the library (it was locked) when Mr. Steadman found us. "We can't get in," Lily told him.

"You don't need to get in," he said. He just stood there, smiling at us.

"We have to get in," Lily told him. "We have to find the bowl. It's our project."

"Lily stole the bowl," I told him, in case he didn't know. "And now she won't tell me where it is."

"I don't remember!" Lily said for the bazillionth time.

But I didn't care. All that mattered was that now Mr. Steadman would see that I was the best helper bee. He would keep us here and we could stay with Nanna forever and ever.

"Is this what you're looking for?" Mr. Steadman asked. "I found it in one of your classrooms, where Lily said she put it." He held out the bowl, and I took it, eagerly opening it up.

"The cookies are still there!" I exclaimed.

"Except the one, and a bite that I ate," Lily said. Now she had a big, big smile too.

"We're going to have to have a long talk tonight, Lily," Mr. Steadman said. "You should tell Piper you're sorry."

"I'm sorry," she said, looking down at the ground.

"Now say it like you mean it," Mr. Steadman told her.

She looked at me. I thought of something then. I wanted to beat Lily as best helper bee so that we could stay here instead

of moving to the next job. But what if Lily wanted to be the best helper bee? What if she wanted to make her dad proud?

"I'm sorry," she said again. As Lily looked at me with soft eyes, I knew she was nice. She had been mean to me for the same reasons I'd been mean to her. But winning wasn't everything.

Sometimes being a good person was more important.

I remembered the day when I first saw her in the office and told her I got in trouble sometimes too. I'd thought we could be friends for that minute. Then the helper bee stuff had happened and she'd become the one I had to beat to be best.

"Great," Mr. Steadman said. "Now, let's go to the office and I'll show you your assignment."

Lily bounced on her heels a little and started running to the office. I frowned as I followed her. Lily didn't want to be my friend. Lily just wanted to beat me.

Later that day, after we'd gone home, I told Mom and Nanna what happened.

"And then she said she was sorry. And that's that."

I ended my story with a big bite of peas. Because nannas like it when you eat peas.

"Well!" Nanna said. "That was quite a story, wasn't it?"

She looked at Mom when she asked that question.

"Yes, quite a story," Mom said. She picked up the bowl and dropped a whole new spoonful of peas on my plate.

The joke was on her, though. Because I'd started liking peas without her knowing it.

"So I got a call from the recruiter," Mom said. "There's a new job. And it's in Florida."

"Ooh, Florida," Nanna said. "That sounds . . . sunny."

"Yes. It's a fun job too," Mom said.

They were saying all this like I wasn't sitting right there. I didn't want Mom to take another job. I wanted Mom to work here forever. I wanted to stay here with Nanna and her great dog, Oreo, forever. I even didn't mind Lily so much.

"I want to stay here," I announced.

That made Mom stop smiling. Nanna didn't stop, though. I saw her look over at Mom and make herself frown.

Nanna wanted us to stay! I thought about that for a second and decided I should keep that a secret. Maybe we could talk Mom into it together.

"I wasn't finished," Mom said. "I didn't take the assignment. I can stay here until Mr. Steadman doesn't need me anymore."

"We can stay here?" I asked.

"For now, yes," Mom said. "But only if you start behaving and being nice. Even to Lily."

I heard Mom's words, but I was too busy jumping up and down. And it turns out, when you jump up and down, Oreo starts jumping around too. Which is cool because it's like you're dancing with a puppy. And who doesn't love dancing with a puppy?

Class Fact #8

How to say you're sorry (and really mean it):

#1 LOOK AT THE PERSON. (THIS IS IMPORTANT!)

#2 SAY THE WORDS "I'M SORRY."

#3 SAY WHAT YOU'RE SORRY FOR DOING. EXAMPLE: "I'M SORRY I STEPPED ON YOUR FOOT." (OR "ate all YOUR PIE" OR "SAID I DIDN'T LIKE YOUR NEW DRESS.")

#1 DO SOMETHING NICE FOR THE PERSON. (LIKE MAKE A PIE OR GIVE HER ONE OF YOUR DRESSES.)

#5 SAY YOU'LL NEVER, EVER DO THAT MEAN THING AGAIN. AND DON'T.

CHAPTER ★ 9 ★

Something felt weird when I walked into school the next morning. By lunchtime I knew what had happened.

Lily had taken all my friends.

Before now, she always sat at the end of the lunch table with her one friend. Now she had people all around her. And I sat down with my lunch among a bunch of empty chairs.

I called out a "hi" to Jeska and Matthew

and Katie. They looked at me and giggled.

So I ate lunch all by myself.

In class, nobody would let me borrow a marker when my purple one ran out of ink. And purple was my favorite color too.

The only person who would talk to me was Miss Cindy. Even when Lily told her she shouldn't be nice to me. "That isn't nice, Lily," Miss Cindy told her. "Would you want me to stop talking to you?"

"But Piper was mean to me about the cookies," Lily explained.

"Is she being mean to you now?" Miss Cindy asked.

"No," Lily admitted.

"Then I think you should be nice to her," Miss Cindy said.

Especially since Lily took my cookies. I decided I should just keep quiet on that, though.

"Let's just get this done for Mr. Steadman so he'll be really proud of us, okay?" Miss Cindy said.

We were all working on Mr. Steadman's "big project." We were coloring a big banner that said, WELCOME, PARENTS! for the conferences that would be held next week.

"I need someone to run these to Miss Nutter's room," Miss Cindy said when we were finished with the banner. It was super colorful. If I were a mom or dad, I would love it! "Who wants to do that?"

"I do!" I said.

"I do!" Lily said at the same time.

We looked at each other, then said, "I do!" together, really loudly.

Miss Cindy sighed. "Go together and make sure you put them on Miss Nutter's desk," she said. "And don't touch anything!"

Miss Cindy handed the stack of papers to me, which meant I won! But I wanted to be nice, so I gave Lily a couple of pages off the top. That was the right thing to do.

"No fair," Lily said. "Why do you get to carry most of the pages?"

"Because Miss Cindy gave them to me, that's why," I said. Miss Cindy wanted us to work together, I thought. I should work with her. I should be nice.

But we were halfway to the room when Lily stopped walking. She crossed her arms over her chest, the pages floating to the floor in front of her.

"I don't want to do it," she said. "You do it."

And then she turned and stomped back toward the office.

Shrugging, I picked up the pages and continued toward Miss Nutter's room. I didn't need Lily anyway. I'd do this and show Mr. Steadman and Miss Cindy that I was the best helper bee. Because good helper bees were nice to other helper bees.

Putting papers on desks was fun even if it wasn't important work. You just walk in, set the papers in the middle of the desk, and walk out again. Only, as I set those papers down, I saw something on

Miss Nutter's desk. Something I wasn't supposed to see.

It was all our art projects. Mine was a painting of a big house with Mom, Oreo, and Nanna. It was an even bigger house than Nanna's, with a big yard and a swing set I could play on all the time.

There were others too. There was Mouse's and Katie's, and even one by that weird boy who sits behind me and pulls my hair when I'm not looking. But in the middle of the stack was Lily's, and it was the most interesting of all.

It was a picture of me with the name "Piper" written above me. I was holding a big bowl of cookies. It was folded up and taped all around so I couldn't see what was on the other side of the page.

There was something mean about me inside of the paper. I was sure of it!

I could take this to Mr. Steadman and show him that I'm trying to be nice. He'd see that I was a good helper bee, and maybe, just maybe, he'd make Lily stop being mean to me, once and forever—and we could be friends.

I was surprised how much I wanted that last part to happen.

Class Fact #9

If you get to do art in school, you're lucky. Here are a few things about famous artists you might not know:

#1 DR. SEUSS HAD A CRAZY HAT COLLECTION. WHEN PEOPLE CAME OVER TO HIS HOUSE TO PARTIES, HE MADE THEM WEAR FUNNY HATS.

#2 CLAUDE MONET IS ONE OF THE MOST FAMOUS ARTISTS EVER, BUT HIS DAD DIDN'T WANT HIM TO BE AN ARTIST. HE THOUGHT HE SHOULD RUN A GROCERY STORE INSTEAD.

#3 PABLO PICASSO'S FIRST WORD WAS "PENCIL."

#4 IN SOME COUNTRIES, ART CLASSES ARE REQUIRED IN SCHOOLS. THOSE COUNTRIES ALWAYS RANK HIGHER IN MATH AND SCIENCE TEST SCORES.

CHAPTER ★10★

"Did you leave the pages?" Lily asked, when she saw me walk into the principal's office.

"Yes," I said.

"No, you didn't," she said. "You're holding something behind your back."

I just kept walking, all the way to Mr. Steadman's office. I couldn't wait to show him. This was the very best thing ever.

It was the thing I'd been looking for all my life. Okay, all the three days we'd been here. But when he saw this, Mr. Steadman would make me the forever helper bee.

"What do you have behind your back?" Miss Cindy asked.

She was over next to Lily now. They were both looking at me. I had to hurry.

I knocked on Mr. Steadman's door.

"What are you doing?" Lily asked.

"Nothing," I said.

"What's behind your back?"

Lily came around the counter now. She was going to see what I was holding. I knocked even harder on Mr. Steadman's door.

Lily was getting closer. If she got to me before Mr. Steadman opened his door, she'd take the picture and tear it up. He'd never see it. Lily would be the forever best helper bee ever. And forever mean to me.

What if Mr. Steadman wasn't in there? What if I was knocking on the door and nobody would ever answer?

Just as my palms started getting all sweaty because I was nervous about Mr. Steadman, the door opened. Mr. Steadman was standing there.

"What's going on out here?" he asked. "I told you guys I'm on an important call."

"Sorry," I said, giving him a big smile. I held up the piece of paper with the drawing side showing. Then I waited for steam to come out of his ears.

He took the picture and closed the office door.

My smile vanished.

"What did you give him?"

That was my mom's voice. I didn't even know she was back there. She must have been way in the back.

"I gave him a picture," I said. "Lily

drew it. It was of me with the cookies. She was making fun of me."

"Was not!" Lily said really loudly.

"Was too!" I said really loudly back.

"You didn't look inside. There was nice stuff inside. Dad!"

She said that last part so loudly, I wanted to plug my ears. She was making my hearing hurt with her yelly-ness.

The door behind me opened and I heard a sigh. Mr. Steadman was losing patience. When I turned around, I saw the paper being held out next to me. Mr. Steadman had unfolded it to show the picture inside.

It was a picture of Lily with the words "I'm sorry to Piper" written right there in big letters.

Oh no. I had made a big mistake. My heart got all melty.

"Piper—?" Mr. Steadman started, and I knew where this was going.

"I'm sorry for thinking it was mean," I blurted, looking at Lily. I'm so, so, so, so, so sorry."

I worried if that was enough *so*'s. Maybe I should add some more.

"So, so, so, so, so—"

"Yeah, we both understand," Mr. Steadman said, but he was smiling.

"Piper, that's very nice of you," Mom said. "It sounds like the two of you can do better working together than against each other. Right?"

I smiled. I nodded. And I noticed Lily was smiling too.

We hadn't said we were going to be friends, but I thought we might be able to. We just had to keep being nice to each other.

♡ ♡ ♡

Saying "I'm sorry" and making up is good. It takes "maturity," my mom said.

My mom was disappointed in me, though, for being mean. Disappointed was worse than anything. I wasn't the best helper bee ever, either. Lily and I both were equal helper bees.

But good news. Lily and I were friends now. We even said we were going to sit together at lunch from now on.

I told Nanna all of this while helping her make stuffing for dinner. I don't really like stuffing, but I like helping Nanna cook. It's fun.

"Do you think you and Lily will stay friends?" Nanna asked.

I shrugged. "Maybe," I said. "I mean, I hope so!"

"Do you want to be her friend?" Nanna asked.

I nodded. "She said she'd let me have my other friends back," I said. "She told them all I was a stinky-mean-tattletale-pants, but she's taking that back now."

Nanna laughed at that. "Well, you're not mean." She leaned over and sniffed me. "And you smell good to me. Sounds to me like you just have to work a little on being a good listener and friend."

"She does," Mom said. She'd been listening to the whole thing, I guess. She was sitting at the table, typing on her laptop.

"I promise to be nice to Lily and to everyone," I said. "Besides, I want to have more friends at school."

"You will," Nanna said. "But no matter what, you always have me and your mom," she said.

"And Oreo!" I said loudly.

Oreo liked that. He jumped up and

gave me a big sloppy kiss. And Nanna was right. No matter what happened, I'd always have Nanna, Mom, and Oreo to help me—the best kind of friends there could be.

Class Fact #10

Getting called to the principal's office is not always a bad thing. You could be called to the principal's office because:

#1 YOU FORGOT YOUR LUNCH MONEY AND YOUR PARENTS DROPPED IT OFF.

#2 SOMEONE SENT YOU FLOWERS.

#3 YOU'RE BEING NAMED STUDENT OF THE YEAR.

#4 YOU LOST SOMETHING AND SOMEONE TURNED IT IN.

#5 YOUR TEACHER IS *SO* IMPRESSED WITH YOU, SHE WANTS THE PRINCIPAL TO SEE HOW GREAT YOU ARE.

#6 YEAH, IF YOU'RE SENT TO THE PRINCIPAL'S OFFICE, YOU'RE PROBABLY IN TROUBLE.

Turn the page for a sneak peek at
Piper's next adventure:

PIPER MORGAN TO THE RESCUE

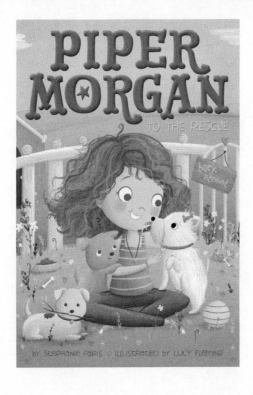

I really want a dog of my own.

I've never had one before, but I've always wanted one. Mom always said it wasn't the right time, but there's never a bad time to have a puppy in your life.

My nanna has a cute little dog named Oreo. He's black and white and loves to have dance parties with me. I *love* Oreo. I got to hang out with him all the time when we lived with Nanna for a little bit. But

Mom got a new job, so I don't get to live with Oreo anymore. We just moved into a new place in Ohio.

My mom has worked lots of jobs. She's worked in a circus and a school. And at each job, I was able to help out in my own special way too.

Now we were going to work where doggies and kitties come when they didn't have homes. Mom said it's called a pet rescue. She's going to help the boss, who owns lots and lots of pet places in Ohio. Mom's going to be what's called an "assistant director."

Plus, not only do we get to go somewhere new, but it sounds like I might be able to be around a lot of really cute animals. It will another great adventure!

I didn't always like new adventures,

though. At first I was scared about going to new places. But every time we went to a new place, I got to make new friends and have new fun experiences. I've performed in a circus with kids called Little Explorers, and was a helper bee at a principal's office.

Today we went to my mom's new job. It's summer, so I don't have to go to school right now. That's good. It means we can work at lots of jobs all summer and then maybe get a new job near a really good school that will be my forever home.

But first, I will be hanging out with animals. Lots and lots of animals.

"Can we keep one, please, please, please?" I ask my mom on the way to the rescue shelter to meet her new boss.

One 'please' didn't get you as much as three of them. Most of the time, grown-ups didn't say yes even to three pleases, but sometimes they did. So you should always try.

Please, please, *please*!

"No pets," Mom said. "Not until we get settled somewhere."

"Maybe this will be our new home," I said. "I like Ohio."

I did miss Nanna, though. Nanna was two hours from here. That was a long, long way, but not too long. Mom said we could still go visit on our days off, though, which were every Sunday and sometimes Monday.

"Maybe it will be," Mom said. "But we're just helping out right now while the owner opens a new store, remember?"

I knew that, but I think I might like this job best of all the ones we have done so far. My most favorite part of the circus was the elephant named Ella. I made friends after that and they were the best part, but I still liked the elephant.

Dogs and cats were even better than elephants. You know why? Because you can have them in your house. They can even sleep on your bed if your parents will let them do it.

I decided this was going to be Mom's forever job. I'd do an extra-good job and then Mom would let us have a puppy dog of our very own. Because life is just so much better if you have a puppy sleeping next to you.